Nanni's Hijab

By Khadijah Abdul-Haqq

This Book Belongs To

_____

In the Name of Allah.
To my Family, you are my every motivation. I love you.
To every young hijabi, may Nanni's Hijab give
you motivation to find your strength in the face of adversity.
To the reader, please make dua for the author;
you are the reason for this book.

Always,

KAH

Djarabi Kitabs Publishing
P.O. BOX 703733
Dallas, TX 75370
USA

ISBN-13: 978-1-947148-81-9
Library of Congress Control Number: 2018900894

www.djarabikitabs.com
Printed in the United States of America

Nanni's Hijab

By Khadijah Abdul-Haqq

Illustrated by Vitchapol Taerattanachai

Nanni loved wearing her hijab and she loved going to school. She wore a different hijab to school every day. Nanni never wore the same hijab twice.

On Mondays, she wore a red hijab.

On Tuesdays, she wore a blue hijab.

Wednesdays were the best days of all because Wednesday was pink hijab day and pink was Nanni's favorite color. She absolutely loved pink.

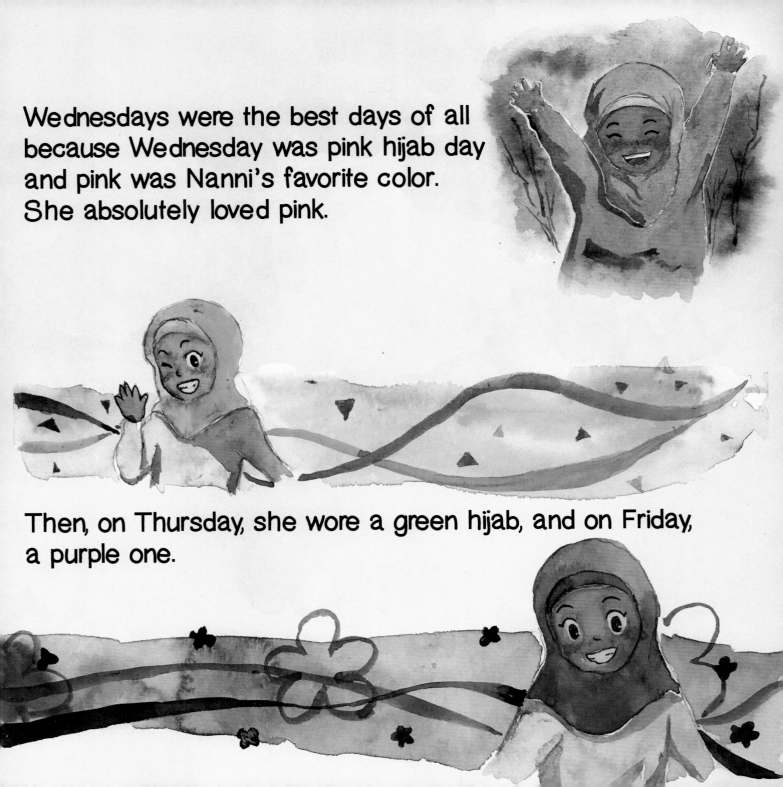

Then, on Thursday, she wore a green hijab, and on Friday, a purple one.

At school, everyone was amazed by her hijabs;
they were bright, flowing, and beautiful.

Her teacher said, "Your hijabs are as regal as a princess's crown and are as vivid as a rainbow."

Every morning, the children sat on the edges of their seats waiting to see which beautiful hijab Nanni would wear next. All of the children loved Nanni's headscarves...except for Leslie.

Leslie was a new girl at school. She sat behind Nanni in class. One day during art class Leslie whispered to Nanni, "I hate your stupid 'he-jobs'...They're not special and neither are you."

Nanni smiled and pretended not to hear Leslie's sly remarks.

At lunch, Leslie spilled chocolate milk on Nanni's blue hijab with subtle white satin stripes.

"Oh, I'm sorry," she sneered, "I didn't mean to spill milk on your 'he-job'."

Nanni looked at Leslie, then she looked at the big brown stain on her brand new scarf.

She took a deep breath and walked calmly but quickly to the bathroom to wash out the stain.

The next day, Nanni was playing hopscotch in the schoolyard when Leslie ran over, reached out... and snatched Nanni's hijab right off her head!

"I got your ugly 'he-job'," Leslie snickered. "Come and get it!" Leslie danced and laughed and mockingly wrapped Nanni's hijab around her head. Nanni was embarrassed and furious.

She reached out to snatch her hijab back from Leslie, but Leslie threw the hijab on the ground and stepped on it. "Here! Take your stupid 'he-job'."

A fire grew inside Nanni and her face turned beet red; she was quite upset. She was so angry, she ran up to Leslie with her fist tight.

"What's wrong with you!...Are you crazy?"

Nanni was just about to punch Leslie square in the face when she heard her mother's voice, "Remember, don't get angry, get smart." Nanni growled as loud as she could.

Then she relaxed her fists, picked up her hijab, fixed it back on her head, and made her way back to class. She was sad, confused and frustrated. She spent the rest of the day sitting and thinking alone.

When Nanni got home, she told her mother what Leslie had done to her at school.

"If you'd like, Princess, I will speak to your teacher about Leslie's behavior," her mother said.

"No, Ummi. That's okay. I will handle it, in sha Allah."

That night, Nanni thought long and hard about what Leslie did. She could not imagine why Leslie would act in such a way. Nanni could not get to sleep, so she tossed and turned restlessly, thinking of her hijab, Leslie, and school.

"I will handle it, in sha Allah," she sighed.
Then Nanni whispered a little prayer,
"Oh, God, please help me deal with Leslie in the best way."
And at last, Nanni drifted off to sleep.

The next morning, while at breakfast chewing her favorite; waffles and honey, an idea came to her. "Ya Allah! I got it!"

Nanni jumped out of her seat almost knocking her plate to the floor. "I got it! I got it!" she sang as she ran up the stairs.

Nanni quickly dressed, ran impatiently out the front door, and headed straight to school singing, "I got it! I got it!"

Nanni paced back and forth, waiting for Leslie while the other children played. That day, Nanni's hijab was the brightest hijab she had ever worn; it was bubblegum pink with gemstones, satin stripes, and a pink rose on the side. The hijab made Nanni feel so good, her face was beaming.

When Leslie arrived, she looked at Nanni and snarled,
"Got a problem?"
Nanni stood silently thinking, *Punching that smirk off
of her face would feel so good, but I won't.*

I made dua for a better way and that's what I'll do.
As Nanni walked towards Leslie, all of the children
followed behind her chanting, "Fight, fight, fight."

Leslie took off her backpack and threw it on the ground, then Nanni took off her backpack, but instead of throwing it on the ground, she reached inside and pulled out the most sparkling, dazzling pink hijab she could find. It was even brighter and pinker than the one she was wearing.

"I have something for you," she said, handing the hijab to Leslie. Leslie's eyes nearly popped out of her head.

She blinked twice in confusion. "What! You don't want to fight," she asked Nanni.

Nanni chuckled, "No, I don't want to fight. But I figured you must not know how amazing it is to wear a hijab,
so I brought you one."

My hijab is a part of me; it's part of my faith.
It's one way I worship God. It also represents my family, my culture, and my community.
Try it."

Leslie's sneer turned into a smile.
She took the hijab and Nanni helped
Leslie wrap it around her head.
"You look amazing," Nanni said.

Leslie turned and looked at her reflection in the glass of the classroom window. Leslie's face began to glow as bright as the sun. "I feel amazing," she said.

"Oh! Thank you, Nanni." Then, Leslie
dropped her head and said,
"I apologize for being rude."

Nanni smiled, "You didn't know any better; but when you know better, you do better."

Leslie agreed.

Leslie loved the hijab so much,
she wore it for the rest of the day.

From that day forward, Leslie was just as happy as all of the
other children to see which wonderful hijab Nanni would be
wearing to school.

Glossary

Allah - Arabic name of God
Dua - Prayer of humble asking
In sha Allah - If God wills
Hijab - Muslim head covering
Ummi - My mother/ mommy
Ya Allah! - Oh God!

About the Author

Khadijah Abdul-Haqq is married and a mother of five. She is a lover of the creative arts including literature as well as her new love, painting. She has written four books, yet Nanni's Hijab is the first to be published by DKP. Khadijah is a teacher as well as a student of life. She has taught English, beginners and intermediate Arabic, as well as acted as a homeschooling consultant. Khadijah has homeschooled all five of her children for the past twenty years; with the eldest graduating Summa Cum Laude from Lasalle University. Khadijah is also a co-organizer and facilitator of the GEM program for mentoring teenage girls. She is currently pursuing her own bachelor degree as well as homeschooling her youngest children. She is originally from Philadelphia, PA, but presently living in Memphis, TN with her husband and three of her five children. You can learn more at her Blog 'Ramblings of an Unconventional Muslimah'.

https://theunconventionalmuslimah.wordpress.com/

Made in the USA
Lexington, KY
31 January 2018